This book belongs to

....

Copyright © 2012

make believe ideas ltd

The Wilderness, Berkhamsted, Hertfordshire, HP4 2AZ, UK.
501 Nelson Place, P.O. Box 141000, Nashville, TN 37214-1000, USA.

www.makebelieveideas.com

Written by Tim Bugbird.
Illustrated by Lara Ede.
Designed by Annie Simpson and Sarah Vince.

Izzy the Ice-cream Fairy

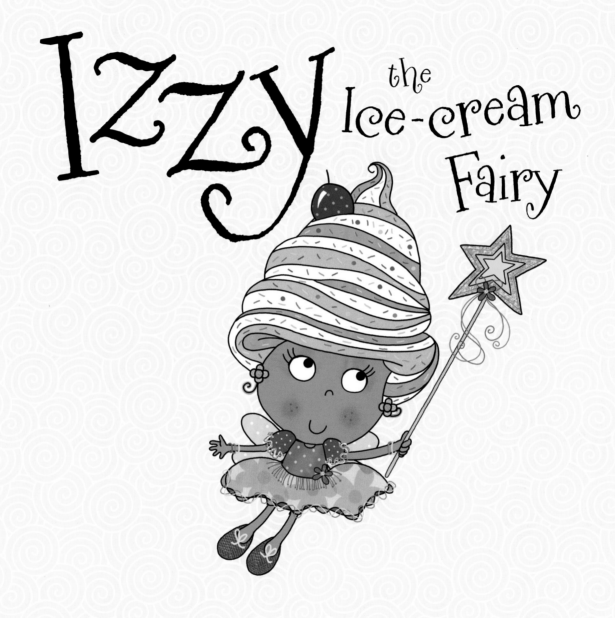

Tim Bugbird · Lara Ede

make
believe
ideas

Once upon a time,
in a **sunny**, sandy land,
lived **Izzy**, Mo, and Mia
at a pretty **ice-cream** stand.

The **fairy friends**
scooped ice cream
from their famous **ice-cream** well
to sell in **rainbow** flavors, in a crispy wafer shell.

And for a treat,
their fairy wands
sent showers,
in all
directions,

of candy jewels
and chocolate chips,
to top the iced
confections.

They saved up EVERY penny to fund their carnival float

and every year, for Best in Show, they **won** the fairies' vote!

Then, early one **summer**, they **peered** inside their well, expecting **flowing** ice cream, but there was **nothing** left to sell!

The well had run
completely dry.
Why?
They had no clue.

But being **modern** fairies,
they **knew** just what to do!

Izzy surfed the fairynet for places cold and chilly with ice cream in abundance, but the results were just too silly!

If you said them fast enough, they sounded almost right, but two made Izzy laugh out loud, and one was just a fright!

"Where can I find **ice cream**?" Tap, tap, tap . . .

"No, that's not right!"

"No, that's not right!"

"**No!**
That's definitely
not right!"

Tap, tap, tap . . . 🔍 ICE CREAM

"Yes!"

Izzy finally found a place
with no palms, sea, or sand.
It was **far away** but perfect –
she'd discovered Ice-cream Land!

Without delay,

the friends took flight

to a place of ice-cream mountains,

with sprinkles falling from the sky

and fruit-filled,

syrup fountains!

"Welcome to our magical land!" said Her Majesty the Queen.

"It's such a lovely place to live, but there's just too much ice cream!"

"You see, it covers everything, so things are getting lost. I'm sure my bike is somewhere here, buried in the frost!"

Izzy said, "That's funny,
our land is **warm** and **sunny**,
and since our ice-cream well ran dry,
we can't make any **money**."

"Can we work **together**? This feels like such good **luck**."
"Grab a **shovel**," said the Queen, "and I'll call

RENT-A-TRUCK!"

They dug and dug and dug and dug, until it was quite clear, their ice-cream haul would be enough to last at least a year!

The journey home was **hampered** by fog and **long**, **dark** nights,

so Mo and Mia
lit their path
with **lanterns** and
fairy lights!

The trip took so much longer
than Izzy thought it would
and as they neared the beach, she cried,
"Oh, no, this isn't good!
The carnival starts today –
whatever will we ride?
It's way too late to make our float,
our hands are simply tied!"

carnival today

But fortune had, for Izzy, one last **big** surprise:

all along the road ahead were floats of **every size!**

The fairies' truck joined the line, with its beautiful **glowing** lights.

It was just as good as a carnival float — a splendid, sparkling sight!

The fairies got to work,
serving ice cream to the crowd.
They made it home just in time
and had never felt so proud.

Their float did not win Best in Show,
but Izzy didn't mind,
for the love and joy that filled the day
was a prize of a better kind!

Izzy, Mo, and Mia made the perfect fairy team, and now they knew just who to call when they needed more ice cream!